THIS BOOK BELONGS TO:

_____

The Wonderful World of
BLUE-FOOTED BOOBIES

Mimi Jones

Dedicated to all who love the wonders of nature.

ISBN 978-1-958985-15-1

www.joeysavestheday.com

A Mimi Book

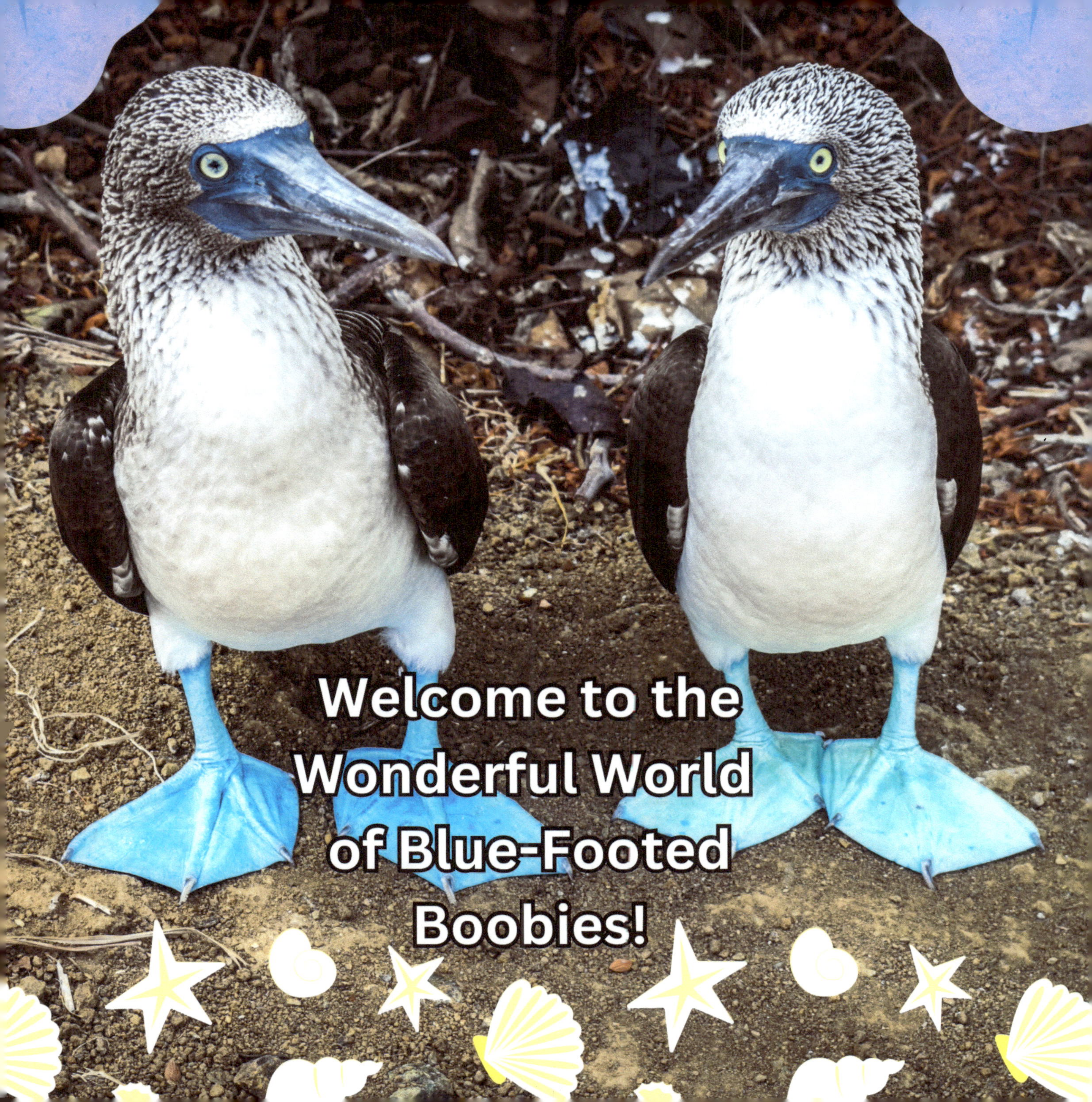

Welcome to the Wonderful World of Blue-Footed Boobies!

The blue-footed booby, scientifically known as Sula nebouxii, is a remarkable avian species that belongs to the Sulidae family.

It is particularly distinctive due to its striking bright blue feet, which are the result of carotenoid pigments in the booby's fish based diet.

These beautiful seabirds are commonly found in the warm regions of the eastern Pacific Ocean, particularly along the coasts of North, Central, and South America.

Their preferred habitats include rocky shores, cliffs, and islands.

The blue-footed booby got its name because it looks awkward and clumsy when it's on land. That's why people affectionately call it "bobo," which means silly or foolish in Spanish.

These birds are well-known for their impressive diving technique.

80 feet

50 mph

They can dive from heights of up to 80 feet, reaching speeds of 50 mph as they fold their wings and dive into the water to catch large schools of fish.

In the world of blue-footed boobies, bluer feet indicate a healthier and more desirable mate.

Male boobies display their feet in an intricate dance, taking high steps to attract females.

Dance

Blue-footed boobies face significant challenges from climate change and overfishing, despite being currently listed as a species of least concern.

Climate Change

These threats are putting their food sources and homes at risk, which could harm their chances of survival in the future.

survive

When blue-footed boobies go diving for food, they have a special way to survive underwater.

To avoid drowning, they close their nostrils using a special muscle and breathe through the corners of their mouth to hunt for prey underwater without inhaling water.

After hatching,
blue-footed booby
chicks have pale
feet that gradually
turn a vibrant blue
as they mature

Around the age of two months, these young birds are equipped with the skills necessary to hunt and take care of themselves.

COOL!

These cool birds show the awesome variety of plants and animals in the Galápagos Islands and other places where they live. They tell us a lot about the amazing world of biology.

We need to protect these ecosystems so that future generations can enjoy and study them.

Enjoy

Earth

The blue-footed booby reminds us of how beautiful nature is and why it's important to protect all the different environments on our planet.

BEAUTIFUL

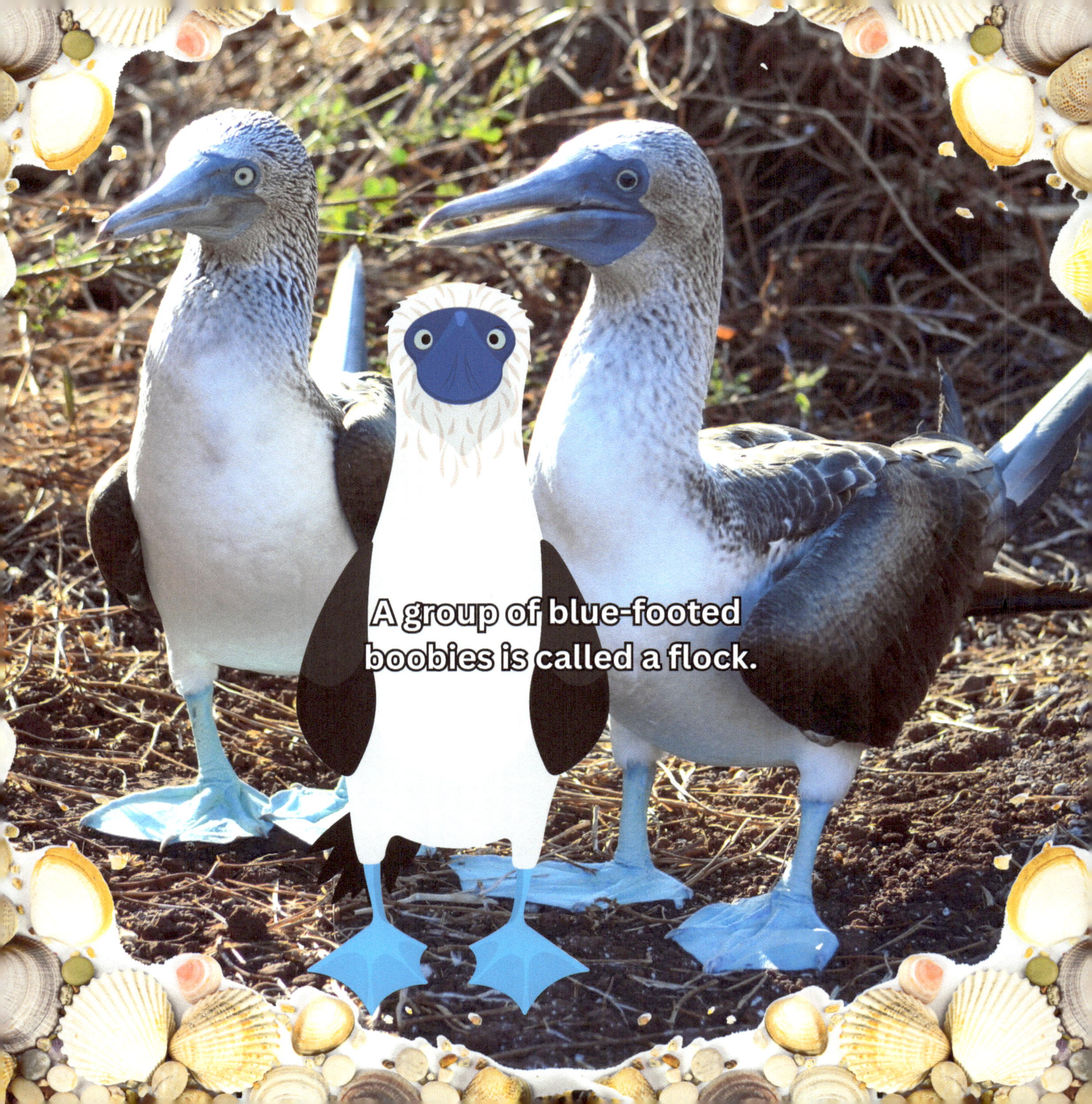

A group of blue-footed boobies is called a flock.

The female blue-footed booby usually lays two or three eggs, with about two to five days between each egg. After laying the eggs, both the male and female take turns keeping the eggs warm.

Warm
A N D
Cozy

While one bird is sitting on the eggs, the other keeps watch for any potential dangers or predators nearby. This teamwork helps to protect the eggs and improve the chances of successful hatching.

Mackerel

Anchovies

Squid

The blue-footed booby is known for its carnivorous diet. These birds mainly consume small fish, including anchovies, mackerel, squid, and sardines. Their diet is rich in protein and essential nutrients for survival in their natural habitat.

survive

Sardines

Squid

Bobby, the blue-footed booby, lived on a beautiful island surrounded by shimmering blue waters. Bobby would start his day by soaring through the sky, searching for the perfect spot to dive into the crystal-clear ocean. He would plunge into the water with remarkable precision, swiftly navigating through the depths to secure a tasty meal of freshly caught squid for lunch.

After savoring every last bite of his meal, Bobby would often stroll around the rugged hillside he called home. As he meandered along, he would pause to observe his companions' distinctive blue feet, finding joy in the way they clumsily waddled back and forth, just as he did.

At the end of each long day, weary from his adventures, Bobby would unsteadily waddle back to his cherished resting spot, on his favorite rock. For Bobby, this rest was vital, as it rejuvenated him for the challenges that lay ahead. When the golden rays of morning light touched the landscape, Bobby would rise from his slumber, ready to embark on a new day of hunting for nourishment beneath the crystal-clear waters.

Can you count the Blue footed-boobies?

THE END!

www.ingramcontent.com/pod-product-compliance
Lightning Source LLC
Chambersburg PA
CBHW060838270326
41933CB00002B/128